Baron Weaver's Game of Bezique

Elle Beaumont

For Valerie & Ashley,
In hopes of not being cheesy—you are the wind beneath my
wings.
Darn it, I got cheesy!

BARON WEAVER'S GAME OF BEZIQUE
Copyright © 2019 by Elle Beaumont.

Published by Crescent Sea Publishing.
www.crescentseapublishing.com

Cover designed by K.M. Robinson.
Interior Design by K.M. Robinson.

CHAPTER 1

"Try your hand at a game of chance," crooned Etienne Mercier. His card table happened to be set up in the market with the hope of snaring the attention of the patrons. Bezique was his game of choice, and it was not a game of chance so much as it was a game of thievery and trickery.

"You—fine *monsieur*! Care to dabble in a game? You could very well line your pockets with a fortune." Etienne's light-green eyes sparked with a challenge as he honed in on a passing gentleman, waving his hand.

"Why don't you get a real job." The man sneered. He wasn't the first to curl his lip in disdain.

Instead of lobbing a quick-witted retort at the man, Etienne let it go. It would do nothing but draw negative attention to him if he snapped back. His lips pressed into a firm line as he lowered his gaze to the card table.

His tanned, worn fingers combed his dark hair back. In spite of living in destitution, he'd managed to scrape together his earnings to purchase more exceptional-quality clothing. Just because he lived on the streets for a time did not mean he needed to look it—or represent it.

He dressed smartly—a white cotton dress shirt, coupled with a dark blue vest. The sleeves of the shirt were rolled up to showcase that he was not, in fact, stealing from the patrons. The joke was on them, he didn't need sleeves to take from them.

It wasn't his fault that he couldn't maintain a job. As soon as an employer discovered that he was fae, they banished him from their establishment. Fae were seen as a blight on the world thanks to the wicked council that ruined everything. It was all fun and games until one diabolical plan hatched, and evil rained down on innocents. Count de Clavière ruined the future for fae-kind, and painted them to be all the same: bloodthirsty, greedy, and willing to enslave humans.

Etienne's parents were victims of a proverbial witch hunt, cornered and killed by a fearful mob. As mercy would have it, Etienne had been at their next door neighbor's playing with their son while they had been at the theater. He had been given the news amidst eating an eclair, only eight years of age, and his world had been shattered.

Fortune had hardly smiled on him. He was allowed to live with the Collier's for a year until they had no choice but to turn him out on the streets. Forced to learn how to pick pockets, swipe food from tables, and use his magic to survive, he had become a savvy street urchin. Etienne had always been bright, and he ferreted enough money away so that he could rent out a dingy hole, buy food instead of stealing or rummaging through the waste bins, and most importantly, clothe himself to set him apart from the typical street rat.

"Come and try your hand at a fun game," he recited one of his several lines. His nimble fingers spread the cards along the table, and then with one movement, the cards shifted into the other direction. As he quickly shuffled them, he noticed he had caught the attention of a well-to-do woman.

Middle-aged, and yet still beautiful, he had the feeling she broke a lot of hearts in her youth.

"*Bonjour, monsieur,*" she offered and peered down at the table. "What is this?" she inquired.

"This is—" His words were cut off.

"*Non,* not that. What is this?" Her hand motioned to him, and she clucked her tongue. She leaned forward and scooped up the deck that he had spread out and shuffled them. "You have to have flair, *mon ami.*" She turned her back to him, her purple skirt brushing against the card table. The white wig on her head boasted of wealth. The curls that dangled from it only seemed to bring attention to that fact.

Whoever the woman was, she had played cards before. Her fingers traversed over the deck with skill, and though her fingers were gloved, they didn't stumble or slip once. Squeezing the deck of cards, they skyrocketed into the air and fell into a neat pile in her awaiting hand. "Attention, *monsieurs and mademoiselles*! Have you ever wanted to feel your heart hammer in your breast? Have you wondered what it was like to live on the edge? Try your hand at a game of chance, just one game…what have you to lose?"

Etienne's mouth gaped open, and he surveyed the attention that had been drawn to them. "Thank you," he murmured as he bowed his head, heat flooding into his cheeks.

She smiled at him. "Take care, *mon ami*, and *bonne chance*."

He blinked as he took the cards back from her. "Wait," he called out as she began to walk away. "Your name. What is your name?"

She fluttered white lashes at him, a curious smirk on her lips. "You may call me Marie, but don't let anyone know that." She lifted a finger to her ruby lips. "I shall see you again, no?"

"Will I?" His dark lashes fanned across his skin, feeling less confident under her intense blue gaze.

She twisted her lips and nodded her head. "I think we will. Paris is not so big, you know?"

Marie, he thought. No surname, no title, and yet she could maneuver a deck of cards as if she had been born in a gambling hall. He wrinkled his pert nose and furrowed his brow. Who could say who she was? The streets of Paris were full of tricksters just like him.

She may not have used magic, but her energy had attracted onlookers, and so he played, or instead, he played them.

Marie had taught him one thing: no matter what, it was always to put on a show. In that brief moment they shared, he knew it was less about seeming like a scam, and everything to do with enticing the onlookers.

Could he take their mind off their woes? Could he make them gasp, smile, or giggle? The more he could, he discovered, the deeper their pockets became. Bezique was a clever game, but so was reading a person and redirecting their attention.

Etienne pulled a card from his pocket and ran a finger along the smooth edge. Notre Dame's bells came to life and told him it was 4:00 pm. Soon, the 4:05 steam engine would be roaring to life. Tucking the card into his pocket, he folded the table up and strapped it to his back before he began to make the journey to the apartment he called his hole.

Colombe Street was a decent walk, but it was one he was used to by now. Etienne kept his hands shoved in his pockets to guard the coins he had earned. He was grateful the steps to his apartment were in front of him.

"You filthy fae scum!" a man a few rows down cried out. Lifting the cane at his side, he was readying to strike down a boy that must have been only ten.

Etienne curled his lip and removed his hands from his pockets as he briskly walked toward the greasy man. The sparse hair atop of his head was slick with oil, and his face gleamed in the fading sun. He smelled like aged body odor and alcohol. Etienne could have sworn he had bugs rolling in and out of the gaps where his teeth once had been.

"Fine *monsieur*, what seems to be the problem?" Gracefully moving so that he could help the boy up and pull him to the side, Etienne flashed the man a brilliant smile.

The boy was definitely fae. The tell-tale pointed ears and too-pretty features painted him as such. It was why Etienne grew his thick hair out—it hid the pointed tips.

"Disgusting Fae; they should have been wiped out when we retaliated. He stole from me."

Etienne clucked his tongue. "Ah, surely they serve some purpose, no? Shining shoes, entertaining the mass-es?" With his hands behind his back, he motioned for the boy to run along. "What did he steal?"

The stout man snorted and waved him off. "Maybe

not even that," he muttered and hobbled down the street. "My watch."

"The very watch in your hand?" he asked carefully.

"I got it back from the runt."

"What a fine watch it is. Where did you get it from? I've never seen such workmanship."

"My father. It was his." The man's features softened as the moments ticked by. He must have been lost in his memories surrounding it, because when he lifted his beady eyes once more, he waved his hand in dismissal and walked away.

When Etienne turned around, he found the boy hiding behind a bin, his large, mismatched eyes peering at him. "Come here, *mon ami*." He sing-sang his words to the boy, and crouched down to sit on a step. "The world is not a friendly place for our kind, but one day they will accept us. Until then, we must do what we can to survive, which either means not being caught, or being clever enough to weasel your way out of trouble." He reached into his pocket and took out some coins to drop into the boy's hands.

"No, *monsieur*, I cannot take this!" His eyes widened as he realized that Etienne was also fae.

Purposely, Etienne brushed his hair behind an ear. "But you could take that man's watch?" Etienne's eyes shone with laughter, his dark brows lifting in mock surprise.

"He was a jackass," the boy spat out. "You're… you're like me."

"In more ways than one. Keep it. Now, run along and don't get caught next time." He watched as the boy scurried down the street and shook his head. Hopefully his words were true and one day Fae would once more be accepted amongst the masses, but for now, they all had to be careful, especially the young ones.

Etienne cast one more look down the alley before he ventured inside the poor excuse for an apartment.

The walls of the apartment were paper thin, so the moment Etienne's neighbors began to crow at sunrise he was awake. Every day was the same, even on the weekends. He slapped a hand against his face and rubbed his eyes. Like it or not, it was time to get up.

Once dressed, he collected his card table, and left for the day. Reflexively, he looked down the alley to see if his little friend lingered around, but he wasn't there. *Good*, he thought, *he was safer for it.*

In the distance, smoke billowed high into the air. Paris always seemed to have a thick cloud of it, mostly due to the steam-powered engines that always seemed to declare their presence with a roar. In the past decade, Etienne had seen the steam-powered contraptions burst to life, and more than that, the automatons that seemed to replace the need for a living being. It wasn't uncommon to see an automaton dusting shelves or retrieving paper, but it was only recently that they made their way into storefronts. That fact stung because store owners preferred to employ an automaton over fae.

Eventually, he made it to his usual place in the market, set up his table, and donned his toothy smile. Etienne took care today to remember the brief teachings Marie was so thoughtful to bestow on him.

His green eyes locked onto a well-dressed man and he flagged him down. "Ah! Excuse me, *monsieur*! Do you wish to feel your pulse thrum in excitement? Do you want to feel as though you were living life on the edge? Step right here; come and play a game of bezique with me!" To his surprise, the gentleman lifted his salt and pepper brows and moved forward.

"Bezique, is it?" the man inquired.

Etienne nodded his head. "Are you willing to take a chance?" His eyes glittered with a silent challenge.

The older gentleman stroked his trimmed beard and strode forward. "I think I *am* willing."

Nodding his head, Etienne set up the table. "What are you willing to bet?" His pulse leaped. If this man were the adventurous sort, he'd put down a healthy amount, but if he were stingy, he'd likely put down a measly morsel, something that would barely feed Etienne.

The man was the former.

The amount placed on the table would feed him for a month, if not more. Gulping, Etienne ran his fingers over the cards and recited the rules and objective of the game. The man nodded his head that he understood, and the game began.

His dark eyes observed the cards even as he lit up a cigarillo and took a puff.

Flick, flip, flick, flip, slide became the pattern. To some, it would appear dull, but not when the players were focused and intent on beating the other.

When it became apparent the man was engrossed in the game, Etienne relied on his magic, blurring the image a mundane would see as he slid away a card that belonged to the gentleman.

As the game wound down, it was growing clear who the victor was, and it wasn't the gent in front.

A sigh slipped from Etienne as he was declared the winner. "I'm sorry. Care to play again?"

The man smiled and took a long draw from his cigarillo. "No, but I'd like to keep my money, *thief.*" He didn't move as he eyed Etienne.

"You're mistaken, *monsieur*, I am no thief." He kept his voice low, not wanting to alert the nearby crowd. It was arduous enough to gain the trust of them, let alone being accused of stealing.

The man snorted, stuck the cigarillo between the

corner of his lips, and folded his arms across his chest. As he spoke, he did so out of the other side of his mouth. "I'm calling you on that. I'm going to give you to the count of three, and if you return the card to the table with my money, I won't have those guys drag your can to the authorities." He jerked his head toward the two burly men hanging back.

There was a reason Etienne was still alive, and it wasn't because he rolled over when pressed by a challenge. His green eyes flicked between the man and the two approaching men. In a blink, he scooped up the man's money and bolted away.

Bellows rang out in the air as he charged through a crowd of people. He felt someone trying to snag his jacket to stop him, but he pulled away. His heart pounded wildly in his chest as he zig-zagged through the populace and darted to the nearest alley. Quickly, he surveyed the area and spotted a rain barrel. He leaped up onto it and jumped for the overhanging roof.

A grunt escaped Etienne as his fingers dug into the roof and his arms worked to pull his frame upward. Once he was on the roof, it was easy enough to leap to the other. He eyed the clothesline below and quickly weighed out his chances.

Just a moment—that was all it took. He leaped into the air, his hands readying to snag the clothesline, and when they did, it sprung loose from the building. His heart fell to the depths of his stomach, but Etienne was ahead of the game, and as the line readied to snap above, he let himself free-fall onto a balcony. It was a rough landing—one that jarred his entire body—but with his neck on the line, it was worth the risk.

With a slight limp, he began to walk inside, praying that no one was home, and for once, luck was on his side. Casually, he milled around the lavish house, his fingers itched to take something—*anything*—but the weight of the money in his pocket was more than enough right now.

A small flight of stairs led down to the front door. He peered outside, and when the coast was clear, he exited. He'd have to leave the card table for a few hours and hope that it would be there upon returning to it.

Smirking, he tapped at his pocket and sighed. "*Merci,* Lady Luck." His gaze shifted too late, and he found himself staring at a pair of bottomless black eyes.

"Nice moves. I commend you for your bravery, but not your stupidity." Somewhere amidst the chaos, his cigarillo disappeared. "Those men over there have flagged down the authorities, but I have to say I am impressed with your dexterity, and therefore I have a proposition for you."

CHAPTER 2

Etienne was still puffing from his efforts, but the well-dressed man scarcely had a hair out of place. Dread crept into the fae's bones—if it was a choice between facing the authorities or listening to the proposition, he supposed he'd don his listening ears.

"I'm listening," he said softly.

The man nodded his head and extended his hand. "The name is Baron Weaver." He paused and waited for Etienne's reaction.

Of course, he was a Baron, he thought miserably. Why couldn't he have been a clerk? Or some wealthy shop owner? Sniffing, Etienne reached for the man's hand cautiously and shook it. Everything in him screamed run, and yet he felt compelled to stay to see what it was this Baron had to offer.

"You may have heard of me, but if not, I run a company, and I'd be interested in having you work for me. You know, as payment for stealing what belonged to me." His head tilted to the side as he gave Etienne a once-over, as if trying to guess where the money was hidden.

No, he most certainly had not heard of him. Although, it wasn't as if he were up-to-snuff on the peerage. He gawked at the Baron and felt his skin prickle. Etienne could give the money back, but he was in dire need of it. "What sort of company?"

"Entertainment."

"What kind of entertainment?"

Baron Weaver chuckled. "Why don't you come and see for yourself?"

Why should he trust him? Etienne had just stolen from him, and yet he was offering him a job? People weren't that kind—not anymore. They would push a starving boy down the gutter without a thought. Perhaps, just maybe, Lady Luck was on his side.

There was a chance that the Baron had never seen real magic before, and, if need be, Etienne would use it to save his hide. He would risk revealing what he truly was to protect himself if he had to. Although, he wondered which fate would be worse: finding himself amidst a hunt or in the crosshairs of Baron Weaver.

Life was but a game of chance, and Etienne found himself rolling the dice.

As it turned out, the Baron wasn't a murderer, and he wasn't going to turn him in—at least not yet. He had, however, taken him across the city to Bois de Vincennes —the largest park in Paris— which hadn't been expected. The park alone was impressive, but it wasn't the size of it that caused Etienne's mouth to hang open; it was the dirigible anchored to the ground. Etienne had never seen one up close before, and he was confident that none looked like this.

The back of the ship looked more like a tower, including several windows and a rooftop, which was actually a canopy. From the side of the tower, a giant sail hung limply, the gold and wine color of the sails matching the awnings perfectly. The front of the ship was also covered by a canopy, and the windows were deco-rated by wine drapes so that one couldn't easily peer inside of the deck.

"You should see her when she's landing. We call her Étoile de la Tempete. Étoile for short." Baron Weaver chuckled.

She must have been impressive to watch, and it must have been even more impressive to watch the workers string up the canopy. Étoile wasn't part of where the shows took place, but she didn't disrupt the aesthetic by being there. A massive tent sat beside the dirigible—the same gold, and wine hue—and ropes tethered it in place. There was one thing that was missing though—the sound of animals.

"No animals?"

"Oh, no, I don't do animals. They smell, eat far too much, and providing food for a menagerie just isn't economical."

Etienne waited for a moment to see if it was a joke—it wasn't. "You're a people-circus?" He pressed his lips together and nodded his head. The furrow on Etienne's brow must have said he didn't understand how a circus full of people could be profitable, let alone entertaining.

A deep chuckle escaped Baron Weaver, and his arm slid around Etienne's shoulders. "Ah, son, you could say that, but we're more than that, too. Come! Come and see. It's early, which means you'll catch them practicing for tonight." There was no room to back out because the grip on Etienne tightened as the Baron pulled him forward.

Idly, Etienne wondered what the park looked like at night and how crowded it became.

"Have you ever been to the *Cirque*?" Weaver asked.

"No."

"How old are you?" Weaver's brow furrowed as he looked at Etienne.

"Eighteen next week."

"Yet, you've never been to this show—or *any* for that matter?"

Etienne's cheeks flushed. "There are more important things to spend coin on, Baron." As weighted as the words were, he spoke them in a cherry tone belying the fact his life had been a constant struggle.

Baron's eyes didn't miss a thing. He nodded his head and motioned toward the open flaps. "Go ahead. Explore *Cirque de la Tempete*."

From where Etienne stood, it looked as if he were about to enter complete darkness, yet as he moved inside of the tent, he discovered how wrong he was. It wasn't as illuminated as the sky, but the inside shone like the heavens on a clear night. Gas lamps twinkled, and torches blazed around the center ring. It was the most fantastic thing he had ever seen.

Above him, two individuals dangled precariously from thick swaths of cloth. He squinted his eyes to watch. "*No!*" he shouted, and leaped into the ring, just as the smaller figure began to tumble down the silks. He reached her at the same moment she hung suspended.

The girl had a constellation of freckles across the bridge of her nose and the largest brown eyes he had ever seen. He couldn't help but notice given that her face was inches from him. Her hair, which was a vibrant red, was held back in a neat braid, she was beautiful—and she was also scowling at him.

"Are you stupid? What are you shouting for?" Like a spider climbing its silk, she pulled herself upright and shot an accusatory glare at him. "Disruptions aren't welcome during practice."

He blinked and grinned lopsidedly. "No. I am Etienne,

and you are?" Extending his hand, he opted to disregard the venom in her words.

"Too busy to deal with you. Get out of here. Take your smooth-talking and go."

"I thought you were falling to your death," he remarked, losing the cocky expression as a genuine smile formed on his face.

The scowl didn't leave her face as she spoke again. "No, I was practically born in these." She plucked at the ribbon and shook her head.

Beside her, an older guy slid down the ribbon. His torso was bare and covered in numerous tattoos—it was hard not to stare. "Is he bothering you, Lil?" His golden eyes flicked toward Etienne.

"No—" Etienne began to reply.

"Yes, he is, but he's harmless." She dropped from the ribbon and padded up to him on the balls of her feet. "Go, now. Get out of here." There was an edge to her voice and a hard look in her eye.

"I can't, I'm here with the Baron."

Etienne watched the two troupe members exchange glances and saw her features tighten.

"Leave before he comes back."

"He'll only find me again—he hunted my hide down before, I'm sure he'll do it again."

She let out a frustrated sigh and slammed her

shoulder into his when she walked away, leaving Etienne with the muscled guy.

"Don't bother, you'll end up with a broken nose if you follow her," the guy teased. "I'm Taurus; you can call me Rus." He extended his hand to shake Etienne's.

Rus' hand dwarfed Etienne's, in fact, everything about Rus seemed to dwarf him. In truth, he looked like an ancient god come to life—bronze skin, gold eyes, sandy blond hair, and tall.

"Be careful where you walk around here—people leap out of nowhere and tumble from the sky." Rus winked and waved as he turned to leave.

Maybe that girl was right. Perhaps he could just go. He could leave the stolen money behind, and the Baron would let him be.

Deciding that was the best idea, Etienne took the bundle of money from his pocket and picked up a rock from the ground. Using a stone as a paperweight, he left the paper money on one of the bleachers.

One more glance around and then he fled.

Baron Weaver was nowhere in sight—praise the spheres! Etienne walked with purpose but did not run since he didn't want to alert anyone.

Ahead, the imposing Étoile's sails began to flap, as if waving adieu to him. Holding his breath, he began to maneuver his way through the park. His foot landed on the road, and just as the next one followed suit, a voice snagged him.

"Leaving so soon? And before we even sit to chat about business?" The Baron clucked his tongue.

"I left your money on one of the seats. I'm sorry, I—"

"Nonsense, I saw how you scaled those buildings, and I also saw you on that line. Imagine what you could do with some training. You'd be one of the stars like Taurus and Liliane. I've always wanted their act to be a trio." He jerked his head toward Étoile. "Let's go talk numbers."

Who was Etienne to say no? He needed the money desperately, and Baron Weaver was giving him an opportunity to not only learn a new trade but to earn an honest wage. Besides, he had a feeling that if he declined, perhaps the authorities would be involved.

Instead of returning inside the tent, Baron Weaver led the way into the dirigible. If the outside was impressive, then the inside was downright extraordinary. Etienne had never been inside a mansion—aside from the lavish townhouse earlier—but he imagined that it would have looked something like this. Teal and silver damask print adorned the walls, but they seemed to shimmer in the light that trickled in through the windows. Curious, he lifted a hand to touch it. "Holy... it's—"

"—Silk, yes, so I'd prefer it if you didn't touch the walls," Baron Weaver said dryly.

Pulling his hand back, Etienne glanced down at a chair that was covered in a vibrant purple velvet. After the Baron's remark, he was afraid to touch or sit on anything, and as they maneuvered through the hall toward an equally as opulent office, he remained standing.

"Sit, boy. Just sit." Baron Weaver motioned with his hand, his brows furrowing.

Etienne's mouth parted as if to decline, but the look on Weaver's face said it wasn't in his best interest, so he sat.

"Whether or not you're interested in becoming part of the show, I thought I'd toss some numbers around. You'd be starting off as a trainee, learning the ropes and strengthening, but even so, you'd be earning at least *this* a week." Weaver pushed the paper forward once he was done jotting down some figures.

Etienne laughed as he picked it up and stared. It had to be a joke, but no—Weaver wasn't smiling. He wasn't laughing either. He just stared, and waited for an answer.

"You're free to go, of course, but that is my offer, and you'll earn more once you're a regular—double or triple that price depending on how much the crowd loves you."

There should have been more hesitation, should have been more thinking on Etienne's part, but he picked up a pen and eyed the man across from him. "Where do I sign?"

CHAPTER 3

I n hindsight, Etienne would look back on the moment the tip of the pen touched the piece of paper and scrawled his name—*Etienne Jaritae Mercier*—and perhaps, later on, regret it.

As his fingers began to loosen on the pen, something pricked him. His gaze darted up toward Baron Weaver, but he was no longer seated in front of him. Weaver had moved from his seat and faced a wall of books, his hands clasped behind his back. Etienne placed the pen down, and winced as a drop of blood fell to the paper, inwardly cursing his luck. *Maybe if he...*

Pulling on his sleeve, Etienne went to rub away the blood, and it only smeared the liquid. In the corner of his eye, he could see Weaver turning around, so he hurriedly pushed the paper across all the way.

Baron Weaver sat down, his forehead creasing as he took note of the smudge on the paper. "All right, my boy," he paused and took the paper as he opened the drawer to his desk. He put it inside and steepled his fingers. "For now, you'll be watching Liliane and Taurus. They'll figure out your training, and you'll be expected to clean up for now. If you have belongings waiting for you back at your place, you can grab them, but starting now, you live with the rest of us."

Of course, when Baron Weaver said *"us,"* he truly meant *"them,"* for he slept in his cozy dirigible while everyone else slept in tents adjacent to the big top. Etienne was accustomed to roughing it, and so sleeping in a tent would suit him just fine.

"That all sounds easy enough." Etienne shrugged his shoulder and saw a slow grin form on Weaver's face. It would have made him laugh if there hadn't been a dark glint in the man's eye.

"It will be something, that is for certain. Come on, let's go see where you'll be sleeping, and then you can scurry off to gather what you need." Weaver emphasized *need* as he spoke.

There wasn't much Etienne possessed that he couldn't carry on his person, but to leave those few things behind wouldn't have been acceptable. He followed Weaver through the ship's corridor, and upon exiting it, Etienne felt his skin prickle again. Somewhere, someone was watching him.

As he lifted his gaze, he caught Liliane glaring at him from across the way, her arms were folded across her chest, and her wild red hair was in a braid against her head. Pausing but for a moment, Etienne sent a quizzical look her way. She shook her head, scoffing before stomping off.

Such hatred sparked in her eyes and all he had done was show up.

"I'm sure you saw the tents before. That is where the troupe readies themselves, and it contains their living quarters, too." Weaver motioned and continued down the grassy path toward the adjacent tents. They looked massive close-up, whereas before, they had hardly seemed big enough to hold a few people. Up close, they were the size of a small cottage.

"The quarters are separated by positions here, and so you'd be..." His words drawled on as they approached the tent. "Here. How fortunate for you only two reside in here, Taurus and Liliane. Some of the others house up to six."

They were tents, consisting of fabric, and therefore, whatever was muttered—lest it was spoken in a hushed whisper—was announced to everyone. Those who had been in their tents peeped their heads out and shot him a curious look. Most of them were friendly, except Etienne had to leap backward as Liliane flung the flaps open. She didn't seem as bristled as before, but the aura she threw off told him he was not welcomed.

"Beautiful Liliane, I was just showing the new blood around." Weaver nodded his head as he stepped inside the tent. At the moment, there were two sets of bunk beds.

Two beds were made, while the empty bunk had yet to be dressed. A carpet was strewn out in the middle of the abode and against the sides of the tent were dressers, and mirrors, too, for when it was time to don their makeup and costumes.

"Have a look around. There isn't much, what you see is what you get." Lili shrugged her shoulders and padded away from the area, but not without muttering under her breath.

A hum came from Baron Weaver, and he turned to face Etienne. "Breakfast is made in another tent. You dine with the troupe. Everything runs on a certain schedule. You'll get used to it, and I'm certain you'll find your company more than willing to aid you."

Was he joking? Didn't he see how chilly Liliane was to him? Or perhaps that was how she treated everyone and it was her standard. Lifting his eyebrows, Etienne scrubbed at the back of his neck. "I'm sure. I'm a quick learner."

"Good, now that you've seen where you'll be staying, I'll send you along with Monsieur Pepin and LaRoche to fetch your valuables." His tone brooked no room for an argument. "They can grab a cab for you." He nodded and tapped his hand on a dresser. "This will be yours, too." Weaver turned to inspect the dresser, a large mirror jutted from the back. "Time is of the essence, son, they'll meet you at the lamp post at the entrance."

Having spent most of his life on the run, Etienne felt the pull to do it again, but, he remained cemented against the lamp post as instructed. This was the first time in his life he would be making an honest wage. Perhaps it was about time.

The sound of hooves clopping on the cobblestone brought his attention to the cab approaching. A man hung out of the door and leaped from it as it came to a halt. "In," was all he said.

Alarmingly, Etienne took note that it was one of the men who had chased him with Weaver. Clenching his teeth, he hopped into the cab and sat opposite of one of the other men who had pursued him. "Don't tell me. *You're* LaRoche, and *you're* Pepin?" The two brutes remained quiet. "Did I get it wrong?"

"No," came Pepin's reply next to Etienne.

It was a fifty-fifty chance, the odds were in his favor.

"Just keep your mouth shut and when we get to your rat's nest, hurry it up." Pepin kept his honey eyes trained out the window, his body radiating animosity.

What a touchy, miserable lot, Etienne mused, but didn't let it color his mood any. Opting to remain quiet for the duration of the ride, he closed his eyes and focused on the sound of the hooves, the jangling of the bronze buckles, and swishing of the cab. When Etienne concentrated he felt the pull of the spheres in the earth—the magic that pulsed in his veins—he could easily touch it, but it had been ground into him to never do so in public. To never let anyone know what he was.

He couldn't say how long he had rested in limbo, toying with the idea of using his magic, but when the sound of the hooves began to slow, he knew it had been for the duration of the journey.

"Make it quick. We've got things to do, too." LaRoche finally spoke, and it was he who pushed the door open.

Hopping from the cab, Etienne quickly walked down the alley that would bring him to his hovel. A grimace appeared on his face as he pushed the door open. Rats nest wasn't entirely wrong, and as tidy as he was, it didn't take away from the fact that the plaster on the walls began to peel away, the wallpaper was long gone, and the draft was likely lesser in the tent than it was here.

"I don't have much," he said over his shoulder, looking at Pepin and LaRoche.

"Good enough." Pepin shrugged.

Etienne made his way to the corner of the studio apartment, grabbed a bag and put in the clothes he had and a deck of cards. His fingers came to rest on a necklace that laid on his dresser. Lifting it, the chain spilled over his palm, and a charm of a faerie hung suspended, a turquoise bead hanging above it. It had belonged to his mother, a gift Etienne had bought her with his own money for her birthday. It was what he was unwilling to leave behind—everything else could burn for all he cared.

Pepin went to snatch it from Etienne. That was a mistake.

Throwing up his hand, a shield formed before him, and Pepin's hand crumpled against it, pain contorting his face. "Never touch this," Etienne hissed. His eyes seemed to glow as the magic pulsed in his veins.

Etienne should have been terrified, and while his stomach lurched at the idea of Weaver knowing, something flashed in Pepin's gaze, the honey-color brightening. *Was he also something Other?* Which made Etienne wonder—did Weaver go around collecting Other-kind as his menagerie? "I'm done here."

LaRoche eyed Pepin's hand and shook his head. "That's it? Ah, well, at least you're a light traveler—can't complain about that."

"Take your last look around here, kid, and kiss it goodbye. The Cirque is your home now."

Home. Etienne hadn't possessed a home in some time, this hovel was a roof over his head, a place to rest and hide in. But was this home? No, he hadn't had one since his parents had been killed. He didn't need to look around and didn't need to say his goodbyes to the place.

Upon returning to the Cirque, the lights had already blinked to life, the sun setting which allowed the nightlife of the city to come alive. Etienne stood on the outskirts as the two brutes moved away from him, no need to carry his light luggage. It was there that Etienne felt entirely displaced, and not for the first time. He did not belong in society, and he found yet again he did not belong here either. He was a part of something and still not part of it.

Maybe this time it would be different. Lifting the necklace from under his shirt, Etienne kissed the flying faerie. "I will try," he murmured to it, as if the inanimate object could respond.

Making his way onto the grounds, there seemed to be more people than Etienne had seen before. They were dressed in costumes; some wore painted smiles, feathers, and gaudy outfits. Idly, he wondered, if he shouldn't be racing to his quarters to dress, too, and it occurred to him that he didn't own any pieces that would match the tone of the show.

The sound of gears cranking made him look to the side. Outside of the big top, there was a mechanical arm, and the gears turned. That must have been how the silks were levered and shifted during the performances. It was dizzying to see the show come to life and there were far more structures than he had anticipated. There were tent and living quarters, and games, too, booths and demonstrations. The Cirque spilled onto the lawn of the park and seemed to devour it, one quirky individual at a time.

"Hey, you!" Rus jerked his head. Unlike before, he was coated in what appeared to be gold dust, his skin glimmered like a gemstone, and instead of wearing an ounce of fabric that resembled clothing, he donned a pair of form-fitting shorts that scarcely came to the top of his thigh.

Etienne's eyebrows lifted as his mouth opened as if to say something. Only a breath escaped his lips.

"You didn't think I'd actually be wearing something like *that*, did you?" Rus thumbed a nearby clown. Atop of the ambiguous character's head was a pink curly wig and a wicked smile painted in red over a white face. Instead of wearing poofy clothing, it donned a pair of boots, leather pants and a blouse that further made it difficult to discern which gender it was.

Imagining Rus in that outfit made Etienne chuckle. "I hope I'm not expected to wear that."

"Gods no, you're one of us. You'll be wearing—or not wearing—exactly what I am."

Etienne had never been humble per se, nor had he ever claimed to be shy, but at the idea of being practically naked in front of a crowd had him balking.

"Not quite yet, anyway, I've got to find Lili, see you after."

Color rushed into Etienne's cheeks as Rus walked

away. He shook his head and continued toward the tent. Pushing open the flap, he ducked inside, heaving a sigh.

A scream assaulted his ears, and he turned toward the origin of it, spotting Lili desperately trying to cover her bare skin. "Gods! You can't just walk in unannounced! Are you a creep?"

"Oh, oh! I'm so sorry," he stammered as he lifted his bag to his eyes and at the same time he felt something hard connect with his head. "I'm sorry! I thought you were outside! I thought...I don't know!"

"That's right, you weren't thinking, at all!" she spat out.

There was some rustling, the sound of objects being slammed around and curses filled the tent. Etienne didn't run from it, it didn't seem necessary at the moment. Since they'd be bunking together in the same tent, it was apparent some rules needed to be brought to his attention.

"You can move the bag now," Lili bit out.

Not daring to look at her yet, Etienne moved the bag to his dresser and took a chance looking into the mirror. Not unlike Taurus, Lili's body was covered in gold dust. She wore bottoms similar to her partner's, and a band of fabric that covered her chest. Dust coated her hair, too, but it made it look akin to a fire blazing instead of hiding it entirely. That suited her, he thought.

Padding up to him, Lili narrowed her eyes. "Watch us

tonight, see if that's what you want to do. Not everyone can stomach heights—"

"Heights don't bother me."

She looked put off he had interrupted her. "It's more than just heights, just watch the show. No matter what the Baron says, you may find you're inclined to work elsewhere."

Was it his imagination or was she challenging him? Etienne watched as she padded from the tent. He sincerely hoped that she didn't try to snuff the life from him in the middle of the night. The fae thought back to earlier in the day when he had first laid eyes on her—a spider, he called her—venom and all.

CHAPTER 4

There wasn't much time to feel useless, because soon one of the various hands came to fetch him, showing him what needed to be done. As per Baron Weaver's warning, he was to clean up after the crowd and ensure that all their garbage was discarded. He, however, had to don a pair of dress slacks, a crisp linen shirt, and a wine-colored damask vest.

As the crowd began to filter in, their murmurs filled the tent, and the various shades of their faces seemed to glow from the gas lamps. None of the troupe had made it to the center of the ring yet, but the excitement in the air was tangible. Etienne might not have been at the entrance, but he could hear the crowd begin to whisper "sold out" as he paced around, picking up the discarded programs.

Five minutes into admission, the crowd began to huff and puff as they grew impatient. Suddenly, the gas lamps extinguished, leaving the crowd in utter darkness. When the lights flashed back on, Baron Weaver stood in the center of the ring. He wore dark leather pants, a wine colored vest, cream cravat, and black tailcoat. A top hat rested on his crown, and he smiled adoringly at the crowd surrounding him.

"Greetings, Ladies and Gentlemen, welcome to a night you will surely never forget. Close your eyes, make a wish, and let *Cirque de la Tempete* take you on an exhilarating journey." He tossed his hat into the air, and it seemed to disappear, but above him unseen to the crowd, a gold hand caught it before allowing it to fall back into place on his head.

There was no mention of magic; there would never be. Even if it were an innocent mention of a magical evening, there were likely members of the authorities in the crowd, and Baron Weaver was no fool from what Etienne had seen thus far. What would the crowd do if they did see magic and hadn't a clue that it was actually that?

Shuffling through the bleachers, Etienne continued to pick up after the crowd. His eyes kept flicking toward the ring with every new act. It was mesmerizing to watch, and he understood why people would come here.

In the middle of the ring, a ballerina danced into view, colorful butterfly wings of fabric danced behind her. Music tinkled with her movements, and although no one spoke during the acts, their thoughts were displayed on the faces, during her the motions. The dancer twirled, crumpling to the ground, and then a cloud of steam erupted. A snort came, and another cloud of steam billowed so that the ring began to grow smoky. Beyond the smoke, a great, mechanical bull erupted, stomping, and looked as though he would trample the crumpled butterfly.

The crowd gasped, and Etienne did as well, but the bull approached the butterfly, bent his head and aided the lovely dancer to her feet. It was a beautiful scene, but above all of the performers, the show stopper was definitely Liliane and Taurus.

When it came time for them to perform, the gas lamps blazed, casting a heavenly glow on them as they seemed to plummet to their demise. Etienne had seen that earlier and still found himself flinching. Heights didn't bother him, but the prospect of dying did.

Of course, the sound of the blaring horns, banging drums and the gasps of the crowd seemed to add new tension to the air, too, as Liliane and Taurus soared above the crowd like they could indeed fly. The mechanical device outside lifted the silks into the air. Rus propelled himself off one of the posts, and put himself in a spin as he descended. Silk unraveled from above and hung by his side. Rus teased Liliane with it, and then they were soaring above the crowd, tangling in one another as they told the story of gods from long ago, and how one had fallen for a mere mortal woman. The show seemed to pass in a blur. Etienne found himself caught up in the thrill of it, and his adrenaline pumped along with the crowds. He had never seen anything so beautiful in his life. This was what he had missed by not escaping to the Cirque? A lopsided grin formed on Etienne's face as he weaved through the throng of exiting patrons. He stood off to the side, and once the last patron left, he was able to move to begin the big clean up.

Etienne blinked as he watched Lili hop from one bleacher to the next as if she were a nymph in a past life. "Hey," he called out. "You were amazing." He sounded breathless as he said it, recalling the way the silks slid over her skin.

Lili turned to look at him, a small smile on her lips. "I know." Surprisingly, there was no venom in her words or gaze for that matter.

"I still want to do it."

She spun on the ball of her foot and walked up to him, still wearing nothing more than two slivers of clothing. "Do you?"

"I'm partial to adrenaline rushes, I guess you could say."

Lili assessed him, some of the hardness returned to her gaze, but her shoulders slumped as if she resigned herself to the idea. "It's too late anyhow," she murmured and shook her head. "I think this belongs to you." She reached out and plastered a card against his chest.

Glancing down at her hand, Etienne lifted the card

from his chest and chuckled. "A fool?" He shook his head and rubbed his thumb against the colorful card. He handed it back to her. "You'll see, *mon cherie*, soon enough you will see."

She placed her hands on her hips, assessing him once more. "Prove me wrong, Etienne."

And he would, he would prove her wrong and work his arse off to ensure he had a place here. Not sweeping peanut shells and popcorn, but to be a part of the show—to be worth something to someone. "When do we start?"

"Tomorrow; it's a free day, no shows and it's our downtime. So, please, have an ounce of talent—I'm spending my free time working on you." She eyed him pointedly and turned to walk away.

Dawn came far too quickly. Lili shoved Etienne's shoulder and then promptly yanked the covers from his form. "It's time to wake up."

Unlike Lili and Taurus, Etienne had spent the better part of the night cleaning the tent and making it look as if nothing had occurred hours prior. He groaned and sat up, knocking his head on the top bunk before he collapsed back into bed. "I'll take that as an omen."

"No, take *this* as an omen," she said and pointed to her face, a wicked look overcame it.

Muttering a curse to himself, Etienne thought *this was it—this was how he was going to die—a redheaded vixen smothering him with a pillow.* Etienne stood up. "Already? What time is it?"

Lili cocked her head and tapped a barefoot. "Judging by the bells, it's four o'clock."

Another curse came from him, he had only fallen asleep two hours ago. "Breakfast?" he inquired.

"It's being made—with coffee, if that suits you—which is why I was kind enough to wake you. I figured you'd be hungry." She turned her back to him and rummaged through a drawer until she pulled an article of clothing out. A black cloth—or so it looked like. "You can wear this, it belonged to...*someone.*" Clenching her jaw, she thrust the shorts at Etienne. "Hurry up."

It took a wounded person to know one, and although Etienne knew better than to make assumptions, he took the shorts and nodded. "I will." He waited until she was gone to change into them. He felt entirely naked. His long legs not hidden by slacks, his slender, but muscled torso also bare. Not a speck of chest hair curled on his chest, courtesy of the fae blood.

Thank the gods that it was still warm out; otherwise, he would have been frozen. It wasn't quite light out yet, so when he moved around the structures to find the dining tent, he was more than pleased to discover a fire burning in a pit inside.

"New blood!" someone cried out as Etienne entered the tent.

Lili cast him a sideward glance and furrowed her brows before returning to her portion of breakfast.

"*Bonjour*," Etienne cheerily said, his eyes glimmering. Moving toward the food, he greedily loaded his plate, ashamed that his stomach was nearly audible even over the chatter.

"You sure you want to load it in that heavily?" one of the troupe inquired, pointing to his plate. "Lili's tough; she's not going to go easy on you."

Shrugging, Etienne rammed a sausage link into his mouth. After swallowing, he said, "I didn't ask her to go easy on me." He moved his gaze from the woman and locked eyes with Lili. "She can do her worst all she likes." He grinned and shoveled more food into his mouth.

Lili huffed and turned her back to him once again, her head shaking every now and then as Rus roared in laughter. She wasn't laughing though, and Etienne had to wonder what was being said.

Sitting down next to the same lady that poked at him, he turned to her and squinted. "Why does she hate me?"

"Who—Lil?" The woman wheezed a laugh and shook her head before patting his bare leg. "Child, she doesn't. Lil doesn't take kindly to newcomers. Once you settle in I think you'll find her warming up to you."

Warming up to him, Etienne thought. He smiled lopsidedly. "I hope so, I haven't exactly lived my life to the fullest. I'd hate to wake up dead."

The woman's mismatched eyes fixed him with a knowing look. "Let me see your hand."

Hesitating but for a moment, he offered his hand to her. "Do you read? My mother used to say it wasn't wise to know your destiny."

She ran her thumb along the back of his hand and then smoothed a forefinger over the several creases on his palm. "I do, and she's right. We're not meant to know, and when we do, 'tis a heavy burden. I won't tell you if you don't want to know." She hummed, and schooled her features, not letting an ounce of her knowledge spill into her gaze. "I will say, you are right. You have not lived your life to its fullest. Take care, New Blood. I'll see you around."

The woman said no more, and pulled away, leaving Etienne wondering if maybe he should have pressed for the reading. His eyes flicked to Liliane again, and when she wasn't scowling in his direction, he took note of her delicate beauty. Could he be faulted for finding Liliane beautiful? She looked as if she had walked from the pages of a storybook—especially when covered in gold dust...a winged faerie, leaving dust in her wake. He also wasn't going to overstep his boundaries, knowing that venom—and likely thorns—awaited him on the other side.

"Ready?" Lili stepped up to him and jerked her head in the direction of the big top.

"Ready or not, does it matter?" He stood up from the seat and chuckled nervously.

Without hesitation, she replied, "no."

"At least you're honest." Etienne rubbed at the back of his neck and followed Liliane to what he hoped wasn't his death.

The tent flaps were pulled aside to let the light filter in and illuminate the inside. From the ceiling hung simple ropes instead of the silks that had been there last night. Squinting, Etienne looked around. Rus was sitting on a bleacher a short distance away, and Lili was currently staring straight at Etienne.

"I want to see you climb the rope," she said, pointing up toward the top of the tent.

"All the way up?" He rubbed the back of his neck, peering up at the top.

"Is that a problem?"

"Not at all, I was just clarifying, *mademoiselle*." He feigned doffing a hat. Without another word, he leaped from the ground at the rope. This wasn't something new to him—he had fashioned ropes countless times with drapes and curtains to escape his foster home when he found himself punished. With his eyes focused on the top, Etienne inched his way up the rope, using his upper body strength to haul himself upward. His legs gripped onto the line.

Once he was at the top, he released one hand, dangling precariously. "Like so?" He tilted his head and looked down at Lili who gaped at him.

Rus roared with laughter and shoved Lili's shoulder. "That's my boy! You showed her, Etienne. Now you owe me a day's wages, Lili." He winked and nodded his head up at Etienne again. "Come down, now. Lili's stewing, but you did great."

Careful not to let his grip loosen too much lest he gave himself rope burns, Etienne made his way down and stood before Lili. She looked less sullen, like she was allowing something other than fury to bubble to the surface.

"Good job," she murmured. "You can climb a rope, and you're not afraid of heights." She shrugged a shoulder.

"I told you."

"That means little to nothing." She didn't snap; it was just matter of fact.

Some of the elation Etienne felt escaped him, but she was right. She didn't know him, and he could have been lying. "You guys don't use nets?"

Lili scoffed. "Of course we don't. When we're practicing something new, and not on the silks, we'll put the net up. Other than that, it takes away from the show."

"Has anyone ever..." Etienne's words trailed off as he caught the sudden anguish gleaming in Lili's gaze. He didn't need a verbal answer; that one sufficed. "Okay, what else?"

Motioning to Rus, Lili moved up to Etienne. She was two heads shorter than him and looked the part of a fiery sprite. "Every day, you'll need to limber up. Working out, stretching, practicing. We'll start with some basics." She motioned for him to follow.

Off to the side, there was a contraption that held a silk. It wasn't as tall as the rope Etienne climbed, but it would serve its purpose. "Today we'll practice two things: climbing and flipping into the silk." Lili walked up to it, and instead of quickly running through the motions, she took her time to show him exactly where his foot should go, and how to wrap it, grab, and push up. Rus fiddled with the silk, so it moved upward. Lili demonstrated again, this time her hands slipping into the silk, and then she pulled herself up and over tit so that her belly ended up landing on it. She twisted to the side, crossing her legs, and perched on it. "Think you can manage?"

Etienne had been mesmerized, and while the last one looked the easiest to accomplish, he was bent on proving himself. "Of course," he said, confidently.

Inwardly, Etienne grimaced—there was no way he

could pull this off. Grabbing the silk, he felt it and was surprised that it was quite flexible—it had to be, of course—but it still surprised him. Holding onto the silk wasn't an issue, it was wrapping his foot in the fabric, maintaining his core strength and pushing off to climb upward.

Etienne fumbled for some time, but Lili surprisingly gave him patient directions, and encouragement. They continued with these two moves until they became reasonably fluid, and his muscles could take no more.

"Good job, I'm impressed." Lili approached him after and gave his arm a pat. "I mean it, I'm impressed. Not many take to it as easily as you seem to. I mean, anyone can get up in the silks, but not everyone was born for it, you know?" She leaned on one foot and crossed her arms.

He nodded and laughed, regretting it because his stomach burned. "I do, but I think that's why I'm here." He didn't miss the frown that passed over her face, and as she went to turn away, Etienne snagged her wrist. "Lili," he said softly.

"You could be anything you wanted. There is more to life than painted faces and empty performances." She shook her head.

"No, no I can't." But if not this, what would he have been. If the world hadn't turned against fae-kind, what would he have been then? It didn't matter. Wishing and hoping for another life would get him nowhere. This was the hand that life had dealt him and the only thing he could do was make it work in his favor any way that he could.

"A simple life in Paris sounds great to me." She eyed him and said nothing more before she stormed off.

CHAPTER 5

The next few weeks passed by in an aching blur. Every day was mainly the same, and every day Liliane seemed to place one more brick up on the wall she was creating around herself. No matter how much he tried to make her laugh or encourage her to let down her guard, it did nothing but repel her.

Anyone else would have given up being civil, but Etienne plastered a smile on his face and teased her like he would any other. All of the other members of the Cirque seemed to accept him, except for Liliane.

It was a day like any other. After breakfast, Etienne made his way to the tent to practice. A blur of purple caught his attention as he looked up. Lili was twirling inside of a bronze aerial hoop. Clad in tight fabric, one leg seemed to be wrapped in bands, and the other was entirely covered. She twirled around, and her body shifted so that she looked as if she were tumbling down. Her strong legs caught her as she reached her hands toward the ground. Lili's eyes fixated on Etienne and a smile formed on her lips.

Again, Lili's body shifted, her hands gripping onto the ring. She allowed herself to fall to the floor the rest of the way. "Have you come for some more suffering?"

His stomach twisted at her words. "Is that what the hoop is—my doom?" He pointed upward.

"Truthfully? It could be, but you want to give it a go? It might be fun." A dark look gleamed in her eye, and the way she said *fun* made it sound anything but.

There was no hesitation in his words. "Absolutely."

Hitting a lever off to the side, the hoop began to descend so it wasn't as high up, that way, if one fell, it wouldn't be to their death. "You first." She pointed up at the ring and nodded.

Etienne lifted himself on his tiptoes and grabbed the ring. He pulled himself up and through before he allowed his legs to twine around the silk at the top of the ring. Lili pulled herself up, and together, they began to maneuver the hoop. She was the graceful one, and while Etienne's movements weren't as clumsy as they could have been, they weren't fluid either.

Lili instructed him to flip over the hoop as she lifted herself up. He bumped into her and offset his balance. He wound up tumbling from the ring and landed on his feet gracefully. Chuckling to himself, he looked up at her and opened his arms. "I'll catch you."

She slid from the hoop, and as promised, his arms

wrapped around her, easing her to the ground. "I can't do this anymore," she whispered softly.

Whatever Etienne had been anticipating slipping from her mouth had not been those words. "Do what?"

Lili spun to look at him and motioned with her hand, but the sound of a slow clap cut them off. For a moment, her walls had been crumbling, and now she carefully constructed them yet again.

"What a beautiful show," came the man's voice.

Etienne had to clamp his mouth shut, so he didn't declare it wasn't for show. His eyes fell on the approaching form of Baron Weaver.

"Just the two I was looking for. I have been thinking, and seeing *that*—whatever you want to call it—it cemented the idea in my head: a new act for the show. We've recycled the mythology story. It's time for another love story, and I think it's time for Etienne to enter the show."

Lili's eyes shifted, and she sighed. "Uncle, I don't think he's ready yet."

Etienne snapped his attention to Lili. His stomach lurched. She was his niece? His breath escaped his lungs, and he felt dizzy. After a little over a month with the Cirque, he hadn't been privy to such facts. Although, if he were to be honest, there were a lot of secrets he held close, too.

"Nonsense, he's come a long way. Put together a

simple routine, the hoop or silks, it's up to you, but I want to see that in our next show." Weaver left no room for an argument. His dark brown eyes flicked to Etienne.

"A month, Uncle, please. In a month he will be ready. We don't need any accidents during the show."

While Etienne felt pinned by Weaver's dark gaze, he managed a fairly confident smile. "If Liliane deems me ready, then I will gladly do the show, Baron, but forgive me for saying if she doesn't, would it be wise to push?"

Weaver's nostrils flared, but then a laugh escaped him. "Perhaps you're right, do what you can in the meantime. Find a compromise, if it can't be done... I trust you and your abilities, my dear." He moved forward and wrapped his arms around Lili, placing a kiss to the side of her head. "I like this kid. If you let him fall, let him down easy," he teased and pulled back. "Get back to practice." He waved his hand and left the arena.

"We don't have—" Etienne's words were cut short.

"We do. If you're expected to perform, then yes, we do." Instead of sounding short and snippy, Liliane seemed out of sorts.

Without hesitation, Etienne leaned down to whisper, "Fly high." He pointed to the big top.

If Etienne thought his muscles were sore before, then this was nothing. Every part of him ached, and they were not yet through with their practice. The hoop proved to be challenging to maneuver with the both of them manipulating it, and while it was only one day of practice, time was ticking away.

"Even *I* can't tolerate anymore. Come on Etienne, let's call it a day."

Standing, every muscle felt stiff. "Only if you tell me something about yourself that no one knows."

Liliane's eyes widened, and she peered around. "Tell no one," she began, and then lowered her voice to barely a whisper. "I don't want to stay in the circus. I want to get out. I want a normal life; to raise a family and be in one place—to have roots."

Hunkering down on the bleachers, Etienne leaned back and listened to her. "Does he know?" he asked carefully.

"No, only Rus, and he would never…" Lili sat on a bleacher next to his head, gazing off into the distance.

Spinning around so he was on his knees in front of her, he replied, "So we will get you out. Get me ready, and I'll help you out. I'll make sure that Baron has nothing to complain about with my performance."

With each word, a brick seemed to tumble from Lili's wall, and Etienne could swear he could see hope begin to ignite in her gaze.

"We have a deal." She nodded and held out her hand to shake his.

"A Mercier never goes back on a deal, *mon cherie*."

That evening, Weaver declared the next stop would be London, and Etienne's stomach fluttered. He had never left France, and the idea thrilled him.

"Only a few shows left here in Paris," Weaver stated as he stood in the center of the ring, looking over his troupe. "Make the most of it. This also means the new shows you've all been working on will debut in London." Weaver leaned onto his cane, his worn fingers drumming on the decorated wolf's head.

"Ah! The English do so love their shows," a familiar woman's voice rang out, and Weaver's lips pulled back in a wolfish smile.

Etienne gawked as the woman flounced her way to the center of the ring and kissed Weaver. It was none other than Marie. She wasn't as dolled up, her wig was gone, and her face wasn't powdered, but there was no mistaking her crystal blue eyes.

Weaver's eyes met Etienne's, and the devil had the gall to wink at him as if he knew, and he must have. Marie must have scouted for Weaver. "So glad you decided to join us, *mon trésor*," she called to Etienne.

Gazing at Baron Weaver, she added, "You cannot run from me, Weaver." Maria cooed and turned to face the troupe.

The rest of the meeting was blocked out as Etienne bowed his head to whisper to Lili. "I know her."

"My aunt?" She blinked, but then her eyes averted his quickly.

"Marie, *yes.* She came to me at a card table." He would have continued to whisper, except Weaver turned his black eyes on him and motioned for him to follow.

"Etienne, might I have a word with you?"

As everything seemed to click together, Etienne felt dizzy, and although he wanted to be anywhere but an office with Weaver at the moment, he had to go.

Mistrust began to build in Etienne as he walked to Weaver's office. He opted to stand against the wall, taking care to not let his bare skin touch the silk wall.

"How are you getting along here? I haven't had a chance to speak to you."

A friendly enough question, Etienne supposed. "Well enough." He wasn't sure how he was supposed to respond. "I haven't woken up dead yet, so there is that."

A chuckle escaped Weaver. "A bit of news came to my attention, and I've been mulling over it."

"Pepin said you're a fae." Weaver sat back in his chair and eyed Etienne, assessing him quietly.

Unfolding his arms, Etienne's body became filled with tension at once, torn between fleeing and fighting. "It's not something I share with everyone, sir." Glancing at the man, Etienne didn't note surprise or contempt in his gaze.

Weaver patted the air and leaned forward. "As you shouldn't. Settle down, this is friendly territory." Toying with a ring on his thumb, Weaver stood from the chair and moved toward the wall. "We've all got our secrets, son." He reached out, tilted a silver mirror on the wall and stared at Etienne's reflection. In the mirror, Weaver's eyes began to glow an unearthly gold, fangs elongated, and his nails started to grow.

A curse fled from Etienne's lips, and he reached for the doorknob to the office, ready to escape, but Weaver's laugh halted him for a split second.

"Relax, I'm only saying we're all something of society's misfits here, otherwise cast away into the gutter, or worse. What you are is not a surprise to me—I can smell you're an Other."

"You're a werewolf?" Etienne dared to ask and wondered if Lili were as well—or Marie—or anyone else in the troupe.

Weaver seemed to have read his thoughts. "I am, although my niece isn't. She's fully human. I was bitten in my teens, and it was a secret my family kept. Still, I was an outcast, and I wanted to do something other than what every other Lord and Lady seemed to be doing." He waved his hand around and strode toward Etienne. "You're safe here," Weaver said.

Everything in Etienne's person screamed for him to run. He didn't trust easily, especially when someone was trying to convince him he was safe—it usually meant the opposite.

"From time to time, we use our gifts to enhance the show—never in a way that would peg us as supernatural, lest one of those blasted hunts begin." He shook his head and sighed. "For now, I expect you and my niece to train for the new act." He nodded his head toward the door as if excusing him. "Oh, and Etienne, be careful with my Lili. That is all."

Be careful with my Lili, Weaver's words played over in his mind. The man was a werewolf, which made Etienne wonder who else among the troupe was Other? Scratching the back of his neck, he made his way into the Aerialists tent.

"Are you all right, Etienne?" Lili asked from her bunk.

"I don't know," he answered truthfully.

She nodded her head. "You will be. Get some rest, we have a lot to accomplish before London."

"Yeah, in addition to that lovey-dovey act, we've got the war of the muses we have to perfect, too," Rus mumbled from his bunk.

When Etienne fell asleep, he wasn't sure, but he woke to

Lili shaking his arm. Slowly, he came to and peered up into her brown eyes.

"*Sonnez les matines! Sonnez les matines!*" her playful voice rang out as she danced from the tent.

Shaking his head, he sat up and began the morning ritual of dressing, groaning, and meeting the rest of the troupe inside the dining tent.

Madame Lucille, the fortune teller, eyed him from across the way. She smiled warmly, her peculiar mismatched eyes gleaming with wisdom as she assessed him. In those moments, he wished he broke his mother's rule about knowing one's destiny.

Breakfast went quickly, which meant he was expected in the tent. Rus was missing, but there was Lili in the center of the ring, the silks wrapped around her limbs as she soared through the air. Without her, the show wouldn't be the same—life wouldn't be the same—and it made Etienne's chest ache.

When she took notice of him, she slid down the silks, descending with grace until she was in front of him. "Ready to work on the routine?"

His brows lifted, and when she didn't say anything, he raised his arm up to grab onto the fabric. Twining it around his foot, he began to climb it, pulling himself up, and together, they rose like two spiders in the same web— and there had never been a more appropriate comparison.

The sound of the mechanical arm whirring to life vaguely reached Etienne's ears, which likely meant Rus had made his way back to the tent, however, at that moment his focus was entirely on Lili. His arm stretched out so his hand reached her ankle as they spun around above the arena. Gradually they came closer to the ground so that Lili could stand and she moved beneath Etienne, twirling in such a way that it just looked as if she were dancing, but with each move, she wrapped the silk around his legs.

Inverting himself, he reached downward, and Lili lifted her arms so he could grasp onto her. He lifted and the entanglement began. Each move brought them closer, their bodies sliding against one another, trusting in their partner.

When the act was through, they slid from the silks still in character, their heads rested against one another, but Etienne tipped her head up and kissed her softly. Every brick in the wall Lili had put up that had been in place before came crashing down around them. Lili's arms wrapped around his neck and the taste of her drove him to madness.

His hands pulled her flush against him, and she eagerly leaped up, her legs were wrapped around his waist. A chuckle slid from him and into her mouth as he broke off the kiss and peered up at her.

"That wasn't supposed to happen," she said breathlessly.

"Maybe not, but I've been waiting for a while to do that…" He chuckled and kissed her chin softly.

A whoop and then a clap came from the corner of the arena, Rus shook his head. "Listen, doves aside, if you two can pull that off in London the crowd is going to love it. Etienne, you've come a long way in a short amount of time."

Lili hopped down from Etienne's waist, her cheeks flushed with desire. "Let's hope so."

"I'm up for more practice." Even if this complicated things, Etienne knew he'd have to let Lili go to live her life outside of the Cirque.

CHAPTER 6

The teardown descended upon them, and it was up to the troupe to disassemble everything. Weaver was inside of the dirigible mapping out the rest of their course, but when the last of the tents were folded up and stored on the ship, everyone flooded on board.

This was yet another new experience for Etienne, his hands gripped the side of the ship as it began to lift off. Not afraid of heights, but not overly keen on a flying vessel, he was forced to balance himself as the machine kicked to life and the sails flapped in the wind.

"Never flown before?" Lili asked.

"Never. I'm not sure I like it." His olive complexion seemed to blanch.

"I'm sure I can find some way to distract you."

Of that, Etienne had no doubt. Lili's barriers had tumbled down into nothingness, and as Madame Lucille had guessed, she warmed up to him. Trust was a part of their act—they had to trust one another—but aside from the act? Etienne trusted her, and that was the first time in a long time he could say that about anyone.

Weaver was another matter entirely.

"Come on, let's head inside." She tugged on his hand and pulled him to the stairs that led down inside of the living quarters. Leading them to a room, it held bunk beds similar to that of the tent, and, once inside, she spun around on the ball of her foot.

It was strange seeing her in regular apparel—not that she wasn't beautiful regardless—but with brown pantaloons, boots, and a simple blouse with a brown bustier on, it was more clothing than he had seen on her in…*ever*. He chuckled.

"What?"

"No, I just thought this is the most clothing I've ever seen on you."

She twirled a red lock of hair around her finger and laughed.

He moved to the window and looked outside as they flew over Paris, once his home, and it was now gone. Good riddance, he thought. It had brought nearly nothing but misery to his life.

"Etienne?" she asked softly. "Are you all right?"

Looking over his shoulder, he sighed and nodded his head. "Yeah, I am, just the first time ever leaving." He sighed and turned to face her. "Lili, I—"

Walkling up to him, she silenced him with a kiss that held more fervor than all the others. "We can talk after." Her cheeks had reddened with desire again and her arms looped around his neck to pull him into the kiss.

Each kiss, each caress of her fingers made the tension ease away, and whatever thoughts had plagued him moments before were gone. He didn't want Lili to leave—at least not without him. Etienne's mouth covered hers, and he walked her toward her bunk bed and laid her down softly. His fingers explored each delicate curve, and soon Lili proved to him that there was more than one way to communicate.

Afterward, Lili brushed the hair from his face, and her eyes focused on the pointed ear. "You're a fae. Why didn't you tell me?" She didn't sound angry or disgusted.

"I think the reasons are obvious," he said softly, burrowing his face into the crook of her neck. "I was about to when you said we could talk after..." He chuckled and pulled his head back.

"Etienne, when I leave—" her words cracked as she spoke them.

"Shh, *mon cherie*, we'll get you out of here." Even if it killed him to do so.

She sat up on her elbow and ran her fingers through his dark hair. "I will be waiting for you."

"I love you, Liliane." He pressed his lips to hers and savored the taste of her.

"I still think you're a fool, but I love you, so I suppose that makes me one, too."

He pulled against him again and reveled in the blissful moment.

A loud bang awakened Etienne just as the airship tilted, and Etienne had to stop himself from tumbling out of bed by using his foot. Lili's body collided into his, and she muttered a curse as she groggily sat up.

"We've landed already?" she asked and wiped the sleep from her eyes.

"Is that what that was? I thought we were dropping from the sky."

Rus knocked on the door and entered. "Wake up, lovebirds, we just landed, and you know what that means."

Etienne surmised it meant no eating, and that they were expected to put the entirety of the grounds together before they could relax again. There would be no show for the next several days; it would be preparing the grounds, testing things, and practicing.

Once Rus left, they both tumbled out of bed and rushed outside before they were beckoned again. With wide eyes, Etienne looked around. This was London? He took a deep breath and smiled broadly.

"Quit smiling and get to work!" Pepin shouted at him.

Squinting at Pepin, Etienne launched himself into

work, hauling the tents, setting them up, gathering up the bickering automatons that would be sitting inside the ticket booths. It was exhilarating to be amongst the workers, but this was more exhausting than the training days.

By the time they were done, food was being passed around. There were still some pieces of the Cirque that had to be put together, but that was enough for a day's work. Everyone was elated to be in a new location and begin their new show—the overarching theme was new love and an untested heart, per Weaver's request. Each act reflected the theme in some way, and together it created a fluid storyline of new love from start to finish.

"Here's to a successful run in London," Weaver said as he lifted a tumbler of amber liquid. "May we all remain safe, and the gods keep us in their embrace."

They all whooped to the toast and drank down their portion of celebratory champagne.

Etienne had lost track of how long he had been with them all, and somehow it seemed as if he had always been with them. The painful memories of his past seemed to blur as new good memories took their place.

When he was finished eating, Etienne began to work on the ticket booth, the automatons were currently lobbing insults at one another which amused him to no end. They each had a way of performing their tasks and didn't agree with each other. Their quarrels always ended up with the lawn peppered in tickets—why or how Weaver didn't tear their gears apart for that was beyond him.

As excited to be in London as he was, Etienne knew this was where he'd kiss Lili goodbye, at least for a while. His fingers tugged one of the drapes into place over the booth, and he tapped on the window, the whirring of the automaton's head made him chuckle. "Be kind to your friend, he's trying at least." He shrugged.

Lost in his thoughts, he didn't hear the footsteps behind him or notice the reflection in the metal of the booth.

"Allo," Marie's voice rang out.

Startled, Etienne stood up straight and spun around to look at Marie. She looked strange to him without powder or a white wig. She had buttery blonde hair and a creamy complexion. "I didn't hear you."

"I know. So, let me explain myself," Marie began and lifted a finger to silence Etienne as he was ready to speak. "Richard—ah, Baron Weaver—knew you were in the market. The last thing he wanted to see was you suffer, so he sent me to scout. I told him a little more about you, and he wanted to see you in action for himself. I don't believe he took you for an aerialist, but he knew you had a quick wit about you." She shrugged her delicate shoulders and smiled. "He knew what you were and did not want to see you become dust like the others."

Dust was one way of putting it. Etienne grimaced, but in truth, he was thankful for Marie and for Weaver at this point. If it hadn't been for them, Lili would never have tumbled into his life.

"To think he wanted you paired with the illusionists." Marie tsked and lifted a hand to run her knuckles along Etienne's smooth face. "I am glad you are here amongst us. Forgive me for the deception."

Marie had been absent for the past few months, and although it was none of Etienne's business, he wondered where she had gone. She pulled away without another word and faded into the milling workers, leaving Etienne gaping after her.

That evening, as the workers began to set the mechanical arms in place for the tent, Etienne was able to see how it worked up close. Once a lever was pulled, the arm lowered the crane's neck, and when it was shifted to either side, it moved in the direction the lever was moved.

Lili stepped over to him and cocked a curious brow. "Thinking of changing your role in the Cirque?"

He laughed and shook his head. "Of course not." Leaning down, he captured her lips between his and sighed. Who knew love could bring such bliss to a broken life?

"Come. Come with me," Lili cooed and tugged on his rough hands.

He peered at the nearby worker, and when he received a nod in response, he followed suit. "What could be so important that you'd drag me away from work?" He tossed his hands up in a mock show of outrage, which earned him a glare. That look tempted him to throw her over his shoulder and run away, but he followed her—and Etienne knew he'd follow Lili *anywhere*.

"Look, same sky, same stars but different." She pointed up at the inky sky which was blanketed in twinkling stars.

Bending his neck, Etienne brushed a kiss against the side of her head. "And from anywhere, it is still beautiful."

"Come with me," Lili said again, but this time the way she said it implied something else.

"You know I can't," Etienne said sadly. There was nothing more he wanted than to follow Liliane until the end of the earth but now was not the time.

"Then promise me you won't wait too long to find me?" she whispered softly.

"That I can promise, *mon cherie*." Spinning her around to face him he kissed her softly, it was bittersweet, and it lingered. "After this show, is that it?"

She nodded, a lone tear streaking down her freckled cheek.

Wiping away the tear, Etienne smiled and kissed where it had ended. "Your tears are touching, but don't you know? There is nowhere you can go that I won't follow—that I won't go."

CHAPTER 7

E tienne spent the remainder of the week helping to set up the grounds for the Cirque, and somewhere in between was able to continue to practice the new routine with Liliane. Each day he found himself tumbling further into the depths of love and unlike when practicing, there was no net to catch him.

Soon, the opening night for London was upon them. The smell of smoke stacks hung heavily in the air, and an eerie fog rolled in so that as the lights blinked to life around the grounds, it cast a strange glow and shadows on the terrain.

London, so it seemed, was more reserved than Paris, for when it was time for the troupe to make their way into the ring gasps filled the air and parents abruptly covered their children's eyes. Most of the performers showed more skin than was deemed socially acceptable, even if it was a woman donning a sleeveless blouse or lacking a corset. Some lacked clothing altogether, but no bodies were entirely bare to the eye—some wore paint in place.

Contortionists scrambled across the center of the ring, manipulating their bodies in ways that weren't natural, and their painted faces seem to fascinate as well as horrify the audience. Weaver's show was not for the faint of heart, nor exactly was it designed for a child's consumption.

It was awe-inspiring, though. Members of the troupe and mechanical device combined created a breath-taking show, and before Etienne knew it, their act was up.

A click-whirr-click sounded off to the side, and the silks dropped from the canopy. Music tinkled off to the side, and Weaver's voice emitted to narrate their performance.

"Let's fly," Etienne softly murmured to Lili.

She smiled in return, sliding her hand along his shoulders and twirled away from him, taking his vest with her in one fluid motion. Lili tossed it aside and strode back to Etienne, her hand lifting to twine the silk around her wrist and he mirrored her movements.

Etienne pulled himself up the silk, using one foot to wrap it around the other and once they were secure, the mechanical arm lifted them above the floor. As it did, he reached out to grab Liliane's ankle, and together, it appeared as though they were flying.

One small tug and it pulled her closer, she moved her body at the right moment, and Etienne shifted his leg so that he could wrap his around her smaller one, and together they entwined, becoming one as the story went on.

Weaver spoke of falling, taking the leap of faith. As he did Etienne and Liliane shifted once more, carefully, Liliane allowed herself to drop, and Etienne caught her, holding her suspended as he hung upside down by his legs.

They swung around above the gasping crowd, and Lili flipped herself upright, gathered silk in her hand and wrapped it around her waist. She tumbled down her silk like the first time Etienne had seen her. She gazed up at him and waited for him to do the same.

He did, and when his feet landed on the ground, he took her face in his hands and kissed her soundly. It wasn't an act—it wasn't part of the act at all—but it felt right, and the crowd loved it.

That night was a success, and London roared with reviews the next day.

There was a new energy that filled the troupe, one that made everyone's skin buzz with anxiety. What it was no one knew—until it happened. Perhaps it was an omen—maybe it was just fate—but during a routine practice, one of the contortionists met his fate.

The troupe rushed into the big top to see what the

shrieks were about. In the middle of the ring, the spindly man lay in a pool of blood. It was the first accident that had occurred since Etienne had joined. It was horrific.

Blood pooled around the middle-aged man, his skull fractured by one of the iron pulleys that held the silks and hoop in place. His once-happy face now caved in, and it was a sight that Etienne wished he could erase from his mind.

"Gods rest his soul," Weaver said after everyone calmed down. "We know the risks, all of you do, but it's why we practice, and it is why we check things not once, or twice, but thrice and four times over if we must. Tonight's show is canceled, we will honor Angelico." He removed his tall hat and held it against his chest, murmuring a prayer.

Etienne squeezed Lili's hand, thanking whatever gods that listened that they hadn't been in the air—or that *Lili* hadn't been. He lifted her hand and brushed a kiss against her knuckles.

"There hasn't been an accident like this in years," she murmured, sniffling quietly.

They were all akin to a family to one another, and some *were* kin.

Pressing his lips together, Etienne pulled her in for an embrace. "Why don't we get out of here for a little bit, see the city—at least one of the markets." He tucked a strand of her red hair behind her ear and pulled free some coins.

"I found some coin for you to spend." He smiled and extended his hand to her.

"Oh, Etienne." Sighing, she pulled herself to her feet and curled into his side. "Take me away."

That, he could do, for a little while and then for a lifetime.

London proved to be less flashy and more practical when it came to attire. While there was still a fair share of wigs, over-powdering, and flouncy dresses, it wasn't uncommon to see the less-pronounced fabrics. There were more shades of brown, and the city in general, seemed to be far more industrialized.

Seeing Lili dressed in attire that wasn't sleek, or, as the Parisian society would see it—*indecent*—Etienne found himself staring. She was dressed in a short-sleeved blouse, brown bustier that teased his senses, and she wore dark brown pantaloons. The light brown boots had a significant heel on them so the top of her head could nestle perfectly beneath his chin while he stood. She was currently glued to his side.

"It's soon, isn't it?" Etienne asked quietly, reading into how she had clung to him on the walk to the market.

"It has to be, or I won't go. I'll want to stay with you.

For thirteen years, this has been my life, and while I'm grateful, I just can't do this—this isn't living."

Etienne's chest constricted as a torrent of emotions assaulted him. "I understand," he managed to say.

"Say something else?" Lili sputtered.

"There will be a day for us, Lil, more than these fractions we share, and together we will live. Find a life for us. I'll find you." Etienne pulled her along through the market and toyed with a few items.

A soft noise left Lili, and she picked up a pair of leather fingerless gloves. Brass buckles adorned the back of it, and she handed over money for them. "I will try."

"That's all you can do, *mon cherie.*"

"London seems like the place to set some roots."

A half smile formed on Etienne's face. "It does, and so…"

"…and so, on the eve of the next departure, we should come to the market again." Lili didn't need to say anything more than that, she would be staying in London and Etienne would be forced to leave his heart behind.

"I suppose that means we shouldn't buy overly much today." He lifted a pair of goggles that magnified the size of his eyes. When he blinked Lili erupted in a fit of laughter, his green eyes lined with long lashes batted away, and he quirked a brow. "What?"

"Your eyes!" she sputtered and held her stomach. "Here, let me show you…" She held them up and batted her lashes which made him laugh. "I guess we shouldn't. I'll only bring what I can carry on myself."

With nothing else to say, the pair milled through the market, picking up trinkets here and there. Etienne came across a crate of metal, he bent down and picked up one of the objects—a skeleton key. He held it up and twisted it around in his grasp.

"Take it, it's junk." The man at the stall waved his hand toward the crate. "It's just scrap, so take it." He shrugged and turned his back to them.

Leaning over Etienne's shoulder, Lili peered down. "What is it?"

"A key." Grinning, Etienne spun it around his fingers.

"I gathered that but to what?"

"Paradise, perhaps." Gathering up the key, he lifted it and nodded to the vendor. "You said you can't take much, but you can carry this." He lifted the key, all he needed was a piece of leather.

A hum escaped her, and she nodded. "I like the sound of that—paradise."

CHAPTER 8

One day—that was all the troupe took off after witnessing Angelico's demise. The memory of his body had been burned into everyone's mind, but if one good thing had to come from it, it was checking things over and not becoming too comfortable with how things were set up. Each day, each show, they meticulously went over their setups, as they should have done.

The next several weeks soared by grievously fast, and when Weaver announced their next departure, Etienne's heart plummeted to his stomach.

"The Americas are next up on the list. They have some neanderthal running about saying he's the best—he's not seen our show yet," Weaver shouted as he slammed his cane to the dirt ground.

"He has animals in his show—imagine traveling with animals," one of the troupe hooted with a laugh.

Weaver lifted a brow and shook his head. "This week, we will be tearing everything down. Baroness Marie and I have a few things to attend to. We'll be back by the time Étoile takes to the sky."

It would be the perfect time to whisk Liliane away, maybe they could even manage to find a flat for her to reside in. This would be a challenge, but the broader opportunity was ultimately freedom for Liliane, and to build a life beyond just a dream—beyond *Cirque de la Tempete*.

Amidst deconstructing the ticket booth, Lili approached Etienne, her face taut with tension. He hadn't noticed because as always the automatons were bickering, and this time it wasn't with one another, it was with him, and how he wasn't properly taking the pieces down.

"He's doing just fine," Lili chimed in.

In retaliation, Otto—the one with blue eyes—shot tickets directly at Lili's face. They harmlessly slapped against her face and fluttered to the ground like feathers.

"Really," she muttered and scowled. "I should rip open your gearbox and fry your circuits."

Etienne chuckled and swept up the tickets out of habit. "He's exceptionally grumpy today."

"Never you mind him," Oyo replied as he moved from the ticket booth. His eyes, unlike his counterpart, were a glowing amber. His movements weren't as clunky as Otto, and if one hadn't seen his insides, they would have sworn he was a person dressed in costume.

Lili shrugged her shoulders and nodded to Etienne, speaking with her eyes.

"I'll be back for you two," he murmured at the

automatons and tossed the discarded tickets into a trash bin. "Wanting to run away already?" Etienne whispered.

She spun on her heel and brought a finger to her lips. "Quiet."

It was clear she didn't trust that there weren't listening ears, and Etienne didn't blame her. Instead, he followed her to the edge of the Cirque. It took him a moment to notice the leather strap hanging from her shoulder—she had a bag with her.

"I thought we could inspect…things." Her words were vague, but they didn't have to be any clearer than that.

"As the lady wishes," Etienne chirped and swept a bow in front of her. She swatted the back of his head, tickling him there. He grunted and moved forward, quickly lifting her onto his back, and he began to run away with her draped over his shoulder.

Lili swatted his backside and squealed as she flopped against his sturdy frame. She ceased when he set her down, her brown eyes wide and cheeks flushed.

"I think we're far enough away now that you can talk." His voice sounded far more somber than it had before.

There was this niggling feeling in his marrow that a storm was brewing, and he couldn't say he had ever felt that before.

"I think you should wait," he blurted out.

"I thought we'd look for a place today," Lili said at the

same time as Etienne. She paused and arched a brow. "What?"

His gut twisted at the look on her face and he scrubbed the back of his neck like he always did when he felt unsure. "I have this feeling…"

"I have feelings, too, and I know if I stay, I won't want to leave. This isn't easy for me either, Etienne."

He reached out and cupped her face, bending his head so he could kiss her lips softly. "It's more than that, *mon cherie*, I can't explain it. I'm sorry, I…"

A mixture of emotions flitted through Liliane's gaze. "Don't stop me. Please, don't stop me from going, because I know myself…and it's hard enough."

Nodding, Etienne vowed not to bring it up again, but whether it was remnants of sorrow from Angelico's fall or something else, he pushed it aside, and together, he and Liliane began their search for a temporary home.

They combed what they could of London, and Lady Luck was indeed on their side. A women's movement in the heart of the city was currently renting out flats. It was as easy as that, which made Etienne's stomach churn.

Throughout the week, they deconstructed the Cirque, and Liliane made trips to her flat, dropping off small items that she could fit in her bag. Meanwhile, Etienne remained behind to help out the others.

"Where's Lil?" Rus asked while helping to fold the big top's tent.

She had been disappearing throughout the week, but it also wasn't uncommon for her to run off to the shops— even in Paris.

"I'm sure she's dropping coins on the latest trendsetter in town." That wasn't out of the ordinary, and while Etienne felt terrible for lying to Rus, he couldn't risk telling him the truth.

"Of course, she'd skip out on the work, the little demon." Rus shook his head and grabbed the folded tent. "She better not skip out on all of this." He motioned to the rest of the grounds that needed to be dismantled and packed away.

Etienne chuckled as he carried poles to Étoile and stored them away. He felt eyes on him as he turned around and found Madame Lucille looking up at him. Curiosity nibbled away at him, and he jogged up to the older, weathered woman.

"Madame, can I have a moment?" he asked softly, glancing around.

"Only just." She pulled a colorful shawl over her head as a cool breeze picked up, her eerie, mismatched eyes looking him over.

How could he ask without outright asking? "There is this feeling I have..."

Lucille hummed and nodded her head, allowing for him to continue.

"Like a thick blanket over the mood here, not just about Angelico—something else."

A laugh escaped from Lucille, and she took one of Etienne's hands in her firm grip. "Do you take me for a Seer?"

While she was the fortune teller of the Cirque, no one had elaborated whether she was a Seer or not. Since Weaver seemed to collect oddities, it wouldn't have surprised Etienne.

"You are," he said boldly without flinching, and in turn, Lucille's smile broadened.

"There is a black cloud about to descend on us. I cannot say anything else. Be careful, tread lightly, and take care of your heart."

That was far vaguer than he had anticipated, and in reply, he scrunched his nose. "There is already a black cloud on us, *what else*—what else have you Seen?" Etienne wasn't going to let Lucille inch away from him.

"I cannot say."

"Can't or *won't*, Madame?" he ground her prefix out.

"I cannot, Etienne. In time you will see." She took a quick step forward and a manicured nail pressed into his chest. "Take care of your heart, because it is your greatest tool." Madame pulled away and produced a card for him. It wasn't a tarot card that decorated her table during the Cirque nights; it was a playing card—the King of Hearts.

Etienne grasped the card. He had a fool tossed in his face twice over and now a King of Hearts. When he lifted his eyes to look at Lucille again, she had already left and was nowhere to be seen. He had the urge to crumple the card in his moment of anger but decided to pocket it instead and stormed off to the tent to wait for Lili.

Etienne had fallen asleep before Lili arrived, and when she did, she crawled onto his bunk bed and kissed the tip of his ear. It jolted him awake, but when his eyes focused on the freckled face, he smiled and kissed her chin.

"It looks so lovely," she said quietly. "It's starting to look like a home…a *real* home."

He knew what she meant—it wasn't a ship. It didn't continuously move, and it wasn't this infernal tent—it was a real place that she could dwell and develop healthy friendships.

"Tomorrow, my uncle and aunt return, which means I'll be leaving." His hand swept over his face, and he struggled with being happy for Lili when it felt like his heart was in a vice grip on the verge of shattering.

"Only for a little while. I know what his trajectory is.

Americas, then back here again. Apparently, the English loved the show so much that even the Queen herself wishes to attend." She leaned down and pressed soft kisses to his lips, peppering his face in feather light touches.

He moved his hands and quirked a brow. "The Queen?" Etienne twisted his legs around hers and bucked his hips so he could then spin her and pin her down onto the mattress. He held her wrists in his grasp and kissed her palms.

"Mhmm…she heard about us—how could she not—and wishes to see us back again." She winced as she referred to herself as '*us*' when she would not be part of the performance again. New energy surrounded her; instead of being controlled, she seemed far more energetic than she had been.

Etienne watched the excitement flitter across her eyes, and he wondered if it was more for the attention the show seemed to be garnering or for the fact she was finally getting her wish. He decided it didn't matter and instead occupied her mouth with his own.

"I love you, Liliane." His words spilled out against her lips, and it sounded less like a declaration of love and more like a heart-wrenching goodbye.

She must have heard it because she began to speak about the plan. "Tomorrow, when they return, things will be hurried and scattered. Amidst the chaos, I'll slip away.

No one will know. Why would my uncle think for a moment that I'd slip away? Besides, he doesn't do head checks."

That was true, for as controlled as Weaver was, he never seemed to scan the troupe for any missing members. Didn't he ever worry about runaways?

"No more talking." She twined her arms around his neck and pulled him down for another kiss, letting her body do the talking, letting each touch and kiss erase his worries and doubts.

Her touches seemed to ease him for a moment, a welcomed respite amongst his mounting anxiety when it came to leaving her. He poured every ounce of his love into this moment—their last moment—for a few months at least.

CHAPTER 9

In the morning, the sound of Weaver's baritone rang out through the park. Etienne had been up long before the sun had peeked over the horizon. He wanted to absorb as much of Lili as he could in their last dregs of time with one another.

"Good morning, Etienne," Weaver called out as he strolled by. "Ready to hit the wild west? They say real card sharks swim in those circles." He cackled.

"I doubt they could manage to keep up with the likes of me, Baron." An easy grin formed on his face. The notion of flying again didn't settle well with him, but he was excited about the experience. His eyes flicked to the automatons that were hauling neatly folded tents toward the dirigible.

Nodding his head, Weaver winked. "I'd pay to see that. Don't go running too far off, we'll be loading up the troupe, and you don't want to be left behind." He hummed a tune as he walked away.

Etienne rushed to find Liliane, knowing that they were leaving soon. He wanted to taste her lips one last time. When he found her, she was hugging Rus, whispering something into his ear.

"We'll be leaving soon," he said, jerking his head and hinting toward Rus to leave.

Rus kissed Lili's cheek. "I'll see you soon." He left without another word.

If Father-Time himself stopped the hands of time so that Etienne could express how much Liliane meant to him, there surely would never be enough time to do so. Every piece of his heart belonged to her, and he believed that this was proof—letting her go so that she could be happy before thinking of his own happiness.

"Gods, Liliane...I'll miss you." His voice broke, and he leaned forward to kiss her lips, tasting the salt of their tears. His arms wrapped around her as he held her tightly. "Until next time, *mon cherie*." He kissed her soundly and pulled away.

"I'll see you soon, Etienne," she whispered and turned away.

Every step he took away from her shattered him anew, but it was for the best, wasn't it?

With the grounds cleared and Étoile officially packed, everyone filed into the dirigible—everyone except for Liliane. The sound of the ship came to life, but a distressed snarl brought everyone's heart to a screeching halt.

"Where is she?" Weaver growled. It was an inhuman

sound that tore from his throat. His dark eyes gleamed gold as he scanned the several faces in the hall. "I said where is she? Liliane!"

The ship hadn't yet taken off, and to Etienne's knowledge Weaver hadn't performed a head count. Perhaps he could smell the loss. Opting not to find out how he knew, Etienne leaned against the wall next to Rus. He hadn't noticed before but in Weaver's clutches was a black feather.

"If I have to ask again where my niece is," he paused to control himself, but every muscle in his face was tense, and he looked on the verge of shifting. "She's not safe, and I know she isn't here. So, come forth and tell me, tell me why she would leave. She can't leave." Weaver shook, a frantic look in his eyes as he stormed toward the door of the ship.

A flock of ravens flew by, sounding off with their caws which seemed to send Weaver over the edge. He ran outside and began to scream his niece's name.

Etienne moved forward, he had to tell the man something—anything—not where she was, or what their plan had been, but she was his family. "Baron," he called out, but the Baron had taken off into a run toward the tree line. "Wait, Baron!"

"She can't leave, she can't leave!" Baron Weaver kept reciting the words, and the more he sad it, the more he sounded like a mad man.

Etienne felt a knife to his heart each time the man said the words, because he felt them, too. He felt them more than he wanted to. Wiping fresh tears from his eyes, Etienne grabbed hold of Weaver's jacket, but the older man turned around to snarl at him, baring elongated fangs.

"Did you do this, son? *Did you*? She's here—I can smell her," his last words came quietly.

The sounds of a shriek rang out, followed by that of another flock of ravens crying out, but they seemed to laugh.

"Too late, too late," they seemed to cackle.

"No!" Weaver roared and blindly ran through the trees. He swore and collapsed to his knees, fumbling after the fallen girl. Leaves clung to Liliane's hair, her dark eyes stared blindly up at the sky. On her torso were several gashes that bled profusely, and her neck had been cut, too. Beyond them a large raven sat, watching.

"Oh, my gods, my Lili," Etienne found himself crying out and crawling on the ground to Lili's prone body. Tears fell anew as he picked up her lifeless body and cradled her against himself. "Why? Why?" he shouted amidst tears, half glaring at Baron Weaver.

"This is my doing, my beautiful, Lili!" Weaver clawed at the ground, howling in dismay, but then his gaze snapped to the raven and snarled. The corvid simply looked at him and ruffled its feathers. One inky feather made its way to the ground. "You! Why, you wretched..."

Sobbing, Etienne kissed Liliane's face, he felt for any life that may be lingering in her body, but none was there. She was gone, his love—his heart—gone.

Weaver lunged at the bird, it flew upward out of reach, leaving a cluster of feathers behind.

The troupe had pooled out of the dirigible by the time Etienne and Weaver returned. An array of gasps went out, and a few cried the moment they saw Lili's limp form. Rus was the first to run up and hug her body, sobbing as hard as what Etienne was.

Anger built up inside of Etienne, Weaver had done this—had known something like this would have happened.

"Liliane is dead," Weaver said in a lifeless tone as if he hadn't just screamed until his throat was raw. "We will bury her properly, and then leave for the Americas as planned." With an effort, he controlled his voice as if this were nothing more than another act.

Etienne gnashed his teeth together, bent his head and kissed Liliane's cold cheek. When he looked up he saw Lucille's mismatched gaze on him, and fury erupted—she knew, she had Seen and had not warned him or Lili.

Carefully, he passed his beloved off to Weaver and decided to press Lucille once more. Etienne ensured most of the troupe had walked away with Weaver and Liliane, and when Lucille was left behind, he rounded on her like a wild cat, his eyes darkening. "You knew, and you let it transpire. You knew." His hands were balled into fists at his side—Etienne wasn't a violent individual but losing Liliane had broken him. "You are a wretched thing, Lucille."

Lucille had the good graces to look away and wept silently. "There are things I cannot say, Etienne, and to say anything would reveal your fate."

"My fate was to live and die with Liliane!" he shouted and moved his hands as if he were about to shake Lucille, but instead he grabbed his hair and sank to his knees. "And she's dead. She's dead."

"It was not your fate, and it was not the way. Guard your heart, Etienne, mark my words, guard it…" Lucille moved her hand as if to touch him, but thinking better of it she walked away.

How could he guard something that he no longer possessed?

Weaver had ensured that his niece received a proper burial, that she was laid to rest properly, and that she was more than deserving of a decent service. Etienne couldn't agree more, but the entire thing was drawn out, which served to shred any surviving piece of his heart.

After the service, Weaver walked up to him and handed him a necklace. "I thought you might want this," he said quietly and laid the skeleton key into his hand.

"The key to paradise." Etienne turned the key over in his grasp, reminiscing on that excursion. If he had realized these would be the last memories he had of Liliane, he would have made them something more.

"I am certain she found it." He lifted his hand and patted him on the back.

Nothing would ever be the same, and when Etienne met the dark eyes of Weaver, he wondered just how deep his guilt ran. It was a demon that did it—so Weaver had later told him. A beast that walked amongst mankind and lurked in London, waiting for its victims. But Etienne didn't buy that, not when he heard Baron Weaver crying that she couldn't leave, or cursing the birds as they cackled in the sky.

Not for the last time, Étoile took to the skies and headed toward the Americas.

Nothing would ever be the same.

C'est la vie.

T*wo years later...*

Etienne's biceps were wrapped in silks, and as he flipped head-over-heels in rapid succession. The silks unwound from him, traversing down from the top of the tent down to the floor.

Just another day of practice, but when he heard a gasp the moment his feet touched the ground, he looked up and saw a green-eyed girl staring at him.

"I thought you were going to fall! That was amazing!" Her voice came out rushed, and although she spoke French, it was rough—as though she hadn't spoken it much or it had been a while.

"Isn't falling one of the best teachers?" he asked playfully and peered behind her shoulder. "Are you lost?" Had she come with someone else—or worse, had Weaver pulled another straggler in?

"No. I mean, yes. I mean…"

"Turn around. Go home. We're not hiring." He didn't growl at her, but he wouldn't be welcoming either. The Cirque was a trap—a death trap waiting to snap shut on its next victim.

"My name is Celeste. Nice to meet you, too."

"Names would imply that you are staying, *mon chaton,* which you are decidedly not." He spun on his heel and saluted to her. "*Au revoir.*" He winked and walked away.

ACKNOWLEDGMENTS

Thank you for taking the time to read Game of Bezique. This story was so fun to write, and I have so much more in store for Cirque de la Tempete. Etienne is a blast, and if you think you might be seeing him again—you're right! So stay tuned in.

I can't thank K.M. Robinson enough, honestly! For making my covers, for listening to me whine, and always being there no matter what. I owe you *so so much.* You're my critique partner and **so much more.** Thank you!

Yentl, I know I destroyed you with this story, and the sight of ravens still makes you die inside, but I love you. Your cheerleading, fangirling, and general love, as well as support, means so much to me.

Christis Christie and Lou Wilham, without you girls I wouldn't know what to do. You're more than a writing squad, more than friends. I love you!

My Let's Sprint girls, Melanie Gilbert, Missy Davis, and Heather Karn—you girls were always there to give me a kick in the pants when I needed it. When I didn't feel like writing we were definitely in it together. So, thanks, I probably wouldn't have gotten this story done in time if it wasn't for you!

PLAYLIST

You know me, I love giving you guys a playlist. Here is the soundtrack that inspired Game of Bezique. You can find it on Spotify under "Bezique" or look me up —Elle Beaumont.

1. The Night We Met by Lord Huron
2. Time After Time by Joseph William Morgan
3. I Think We're Alone Now by Hidden Citizens
4. Forfeit Tomorrow by Citizen Shade
5. Skinny Love by Birdy
6. L'amour Toujours by Gigi D'Agostino
7. Paint It, Black by Ciara
8. Suns and Stars by Really Slow Motion
9. Rewrite The Stars by James Arthur
10. Black and Blue by Clinton Washington

ABOUT AUTHOR

Elle was born and raised in Southeastern, Massachusetts in a little farm town by the harbor. She grew up fascinated with all things whimsical and a strong love for animals. As she grew, so did her passion for reading and writing. Although she prefers devouring all genres, she largely enjoys dark fantasy.

www.ellebeaumontbooks.com
facebook.com/ellebeaumontbooks
instagram.com/ellebeaumontbooks
twitter.com/ellebeaumont

VEILED ALLUREMENT

When Faye, the ruling goddess of Alindor, and Lady of Light, is cast from the heavens by her wicked sisters, Nymiane and Etain, she finds herself unable to tap into her powers. As if that wasn't cruel enough, she quickly discovers that a mask has been sealed against her face, unable to be removed.

She is soon feeling panicked, but as luck would have it two good samaritans scoop her up and whisk her away to a house full of ladies. There, Faye is forced to lie about who she is and where she is from and finds herself easily making friends with her new housemates.

· · ·

As things begin to settle into a new routine, no one anticipates Faye being abducted by King Zev of Melothra, or that he plans to use her as an instrument of chaos, courtesy of Nymiane, on the eve of his annual ball.

A war is about to break out and when the clock strikes midnight-who will survive?

Now Available!

HUNTER'S TRUCE

The Big Bad Wolf never killed for fun—he was on a mission.

Little pig, little pig, let me come in. I'll huff, and I'll puff, and I'll blow your house in. We're tired of death, of prejudice and more, if you don't make some changes I'll kick down your door.

When Niklaus von Brandt's mother is murdered by a poacher it moves him to make a change in the kingdom of Abendrot. Once a kingdom founded by werewolves, it is now ruled by humans who have one goal: eradicate the werewolves. In order to protect what is left of his family, he must make an important decision, one that leads him to become an assassin, and the shadow the kingdom murmurs about.

Too bad the royal family has a secret—a secret that Niklaus plans on using to his advantage, and in the meantime he has given King Ansgar three chances before he comes huffing and puffing.

Now Available!

BROTHERHOOD OF THE SEA

Eighteen-year-old Jagger and his older brother, Kriegen, are recent graduates from Selith Academy—an elite school for Merfolk. The two work to help their community after tragedy befell their father, but when the Uplanders break a promise, the two mermen only have one goal—keep the Merfolk safe at any cost.

When the brothers are divided in their responses, they quickly learn that every choice has a consequence, and every action has a price.

How far is too far when it comes to sacrifice under the sea?

Now Available!

BINDING OF THE SEA

Selith Academy trains elite Merfolk in perfecting their magical abilities, hosting a Trial every twelve years. When Zinnia—one of their most gifted students—and her friend, Dru witness Prince Loch threatening an infamous Sea Witch for his magical abilities despite the royal family hosting the upcoming Trial, they start an investigation that will uncover buried truths and jeopardize the entire kingdom.

Zinnia and Dru will find help from an unexpected source as they use their magic to help bind evil back into the depths when they find themselves at the forefront of the battle that has surfaced after four centuries.

. . .

Will the sea's buried truth destroy them all?

Now Available!